welcome to the world of

Geronimo Stilton

The Editorial Staff of
The Rodent's Gazette

1. Linda Thinslice
2. Sweetie Cheesetriangle
3. Ratella Redfur
4. Soya Mousehao
5. Cheesita de la Pampa
6. Mouseanna Mousetti
7. Yale Youngmouse
8. Toni Tinypaw
9. Tina Spicytail
10. Maximilian Mousemower
11. Valerie Vole
12. Trap Stilton
13. Branwen Musclemouse
14. Zeppola Zap
15. Merenguita Gingermouse
16. Ratsy O'Shea
17. Rodentrick Roundrat
18. Teddy von Muffler
19. Thea Stilton
20. Erronea Misprint
21. Pinky Pick
22. Ya-ya O'Cheddar
23. Mousella MacMouser
24. Kreamy O'Cheddar
25. Blasco Tabasco
26. Toffie Sugarsweet
27. Tylerat Truemouse
28. Larry Keys
29. Michael Mouse
30. Geronimo Stilton
31. Benjamin Stilton
32. Briette Finerat
33. Raclette Finerat

Geronimo Stilton
A learned and brainy
mouse; editor of
The Rodent's Gazette

Thea Stilton
Geronimo's sister and
special correspondent at
The Rodent's Gazette

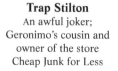

Trap Stilton
An awful joker;
Geronimo's cousin and
owner of the store
Cheap Junk for Less

Benjamin Stilton
A sweet and loving
nine-year-old mouse;
Geronimo's favorite
nephew

Geronimo Stilton

CAT AND MOUSE
in a
HAUNTED HOUSE

PUFFIN

PUFFIN BOOKS

Published by the Penguin Group
Penguin Books Ltd, 80 Strand, London WC2R 0RL, England
Penguin Group (USA) Inc., 375 Hudson Street, New York, New York 10014, USA
Penguin Group (Canada), 90 Eglinton Avenue East, Suite 700, Toronto, Ontario, Canada M4P 2Y3
(a division of Pearson Penguin Canada Inc.)
Penguin Ireland, 25 St Stephen's Green, Dublin 2, Ireland (a division of Penguin Books Ltd)
Penguin Group (Australia), 250 Camberwell Road, Camberwell, Victoria 3124, Australia
(a division of Pearson Australia Group Pty Ltd)
Penguin Books India Pvt Ltd, 11 Community Centre, Panchsheel Park, New Delhi – 110 017, India
Penguin Group (NZ), 67 Apollo Drive, Rosedale, Auckland 0632, New Zealand
(a division of Pearson New Zealand Ltd)
Penguin Books (South Africa) (Pty) Ltd, Block D, Rosebank Office Park, 181 Jan Smuts Avenue,
Parktown North, Gauteng 2193, South Africa
Penguin Books Ltd, Registered Offices: 80 Strand, London WC2R 0RL, England

puffinbooks.com

English-language edition first published in Great Britain by Scholastic Children's Books 2004
This edition published in Great Britain in Puffin Books 2012
001 – 10 9 8 7 6 5 4 3 2 1

Geronimo Stilton names, characters and related indicia are copyright, trademark and exclusive
license of Atlantyca S.p.A. All Rights Reserved.
The moral right of the author has been asserted

Text by Geronimo Stilton
Original cover by Lorenzo Chiavini, revised by Giuseppe Ferrario
Illustrations by Lorenzo Chiavini, Roberto Ronchi and Mark Nithael
Graphics by Merenguita Gingermouse, Angela Simone, Benedetta Galante and Ratsy O'Shea
Special thanks to Kathryn Cristaldi
Original US cover design by Ursula Albano
Interior layout by Kay Petronio
Text, illustrations and English translation copyright © 2000, 2004,
Edizioni Piemme S.p.A., via Tiziano 32 - 20145 Milano – Italy

International Rights copyright © Atlantyca S.p.A., via Leopardi 8, 20123 Milano – Italy

Original title: *Il castello di Zampaciccia Zanzamiao*
Based on an original idea by Elisabetta Dami
www.geronimostilton.com/uk

*Stilton is the name of a famous English cheese. It is a registered trademark of the
Stilton Cheesemakers' Association. For more information go to www.stiltoncheese.com*

British Library Cataloguing in Publication Data
A CIP catalogue record for this book is available from the British Library

ISBN: 978–0–141–34120–0

Printed by Graphicom, Italy

www.greenpenguin.co.uk

MIX
Paper from
responsible sources
FSC
www.fsc.org   FSC™ C018179

Penguin Books is committed to a sustainable
future for our business, our readers and our
planet. This book is made from paper certified
by the Forest Stewardship Council.

IT WAS A FOGGY OCTOBER NIGHT . . .

It was a foggy October night. Oh, how I wished I was home in my comfy mouse hole! It was the perfect night to curl up with a good book and a cup of hot cheddar.

But I wasn't at home. I wish I could say I was bowling down at Lucky Paw Lanes. Or nibbling on a delicious dinner at my favorite French restaurant, Le Squeakery. But I was far away from every mouse I knew. I was stuck in the middle of the DARK FOREST! Do you want to know why?

Let me tell you. . . .

Oh, but first let me introduce myself.

My name is Stilton, *Geronimo Stilton.*

I live in New Mouse City, where I run a newspaper. Yes, that's right, I am a newspaper mouse. I publish a paper called *The Rodent's Gazette*. It is the most popular paper on Mouse Island! Our only competition is *The Daily Rat*. But that's another story.

Let's see, where was I? Oh, yes, how I got to the Dark Forest. Well, I had left New Mouse City to go visit my aunt Sweetfur. She was on vacation in the Pleasant Paw Hills. To get there, I had to drive through the Dark Forest. Have you ever been there? It reminds me of the woods where Hansel and Gretel Mouse get lost. Very dark and spooky.

I had just passed Cat Claw Rock when a **foggy** cloud settled over my car. I felt like one of the Three Blind Mice. I couldn't see

my own paw in front of my snout! I tried to check out my map, but it was no use. I was lost!

The road grew narrow and finally led to a dirt path. Stale Swiss rolls! This didn't look good. Now I was really in the middle of nowhere. I shivered.

Who knows what kinds of crazy rats lived out here in the deep, dark woods? What if they jumped on my car? What if they jumped on *me*?

With shaking paws, I tried dialing my sister, Thea. Rats! I couldn't get a signal on my cell phone.

Oh, how I wished I was home!

I drove on for another half hour in the thickening fog.

I tried turning on my radio to get my mind off things, but I couldn't get a station.

Instead, I listened to my teeth chattering.

Then suddenly, out of the fog, a sign appeared. It read:

To Cannycat Castle

Too shocked to squeak, I checked my map.

Strange, very strange, I thought. There was no **castle** listed.

I folded the map and shoved it into my coat pocket. Well, there was only one thing to do. I headed for the castle. I would ask for directions there.

Just then, a **BOLT OF LIGHTNING** streaked down right next to me! For a split second, the Dark Forest glowed. It reminded me of the time my uncle Flickrat turned on the lights before the movie was over at the Grand Squeak Cinema. The audience went crazy. Every mouse wanted his or her money back. After that, Uncle Flickrat got stuck working the cheese-popcorn machine. His boss wouldn't let him near a light switch.

I blinked my eyes in the bright white light. I could just make out the shape of a weathered **old castle** in the distance.

Right at that very moment, my car stopped!

I groaned. This was just not my day or night. I hopped out of the car.

Now what? I knew next to nothing about cars. I have trouble pumping my own gas!

Suddenly, it started to rain. My whiskers were soon **DRIPPING** with water. And it was bitterly cold.

I turned up my collar and started along the path leading to the castle.

PLINK! PLINK! PLINK! PLINK! PLINK! PLINK! PLINK! PLINK! PLINK! PLINK!

It was covered with dried twigs that crackled under my paws. The grass surrounding the castle looked like it hadn't been mowed in years.

Overgrown bushes lined the walls. *This place really needs a good lawn service,* I thought. Maybe I could give the owners my cousin Greenpaws's business card. He cut lawns for a living. "Next to yellow, green is my favorite color," he liked to say.

Staring up at the dark castle, I stumbled over more twigs. Maybe there was another reason why this place was a mess.

Maybe the castle was empty.

A Castle with Blood-Red Windows

The castle was surrounded by a deep moat filled with slimy green water.

I stared at the building. The walls were made of huge SQUARE stones. Windows protected by THICK iron bars stared back at me. I flinched. The windowpanes were BLOOD-RED!

Just then, a light came on in the highest tower. In the darkness, it looked like the glowing eye of a terrifying monster!

Oh, how I wished I was home! My fur stood on end from fright.

As quickly as it had turned on, the light flicked off again! It was then that I noticed the flag hanging from the castle's highest

tower. It showed a picture of a **bloob-reb cat!** The cat's back was arched and its claws were drawn.

In front of the entrance stood two cat statues. The cats' jaws were set in evil snarls. I gasped. All of these cats were beginning to give me the creeps. Was this the homeowners' way of scaring away the riffrats? Well, I guess it was cheaper than an alarm system.

I studied the statues. One of them had a sign with instructions for the doorbell. It read:

> **PRESS YOUR PAW HERE...**
> **IF YOU HAVE NO FEAR!**

I looked closer. The doorbell was blood-red! **SHIVERING**, I pressed the ringer.

MEEOOOOOWWW!!!

A horrifying meowing filled my ears. Terrified, I scurried behind a bush.

Holey cheese! This cat must be some **monster!**

After a while, I peeked out from my hiding place. Strange, very strange. Not a furry face in sight. Finally, I realized the meowing was *taped*! It was coming from the bell!

Once again, I approached the door. It opened, as if by magic.

By now, I wasn't exactly dying to go in. In fact, you could say I was dying to scurry on out of there!

But then a **BOLT OF LIGHTNING** practically took off my paw.

Yikes! I didn't want to go inside, but I

couldn't stay outside in the storm.

I practiced my deep-breathing exercises.
Then I tiptoed inside.

Crusty cheese slices!

It was so **DARK** and **SPOOKY**.

Oh, how I wished I was home!

I'm Too Fond of My Whiskers!

Teeth chattering, I entered a dark and **GLOOMY** hall.

Suddenly, another bolt of lightning struck close by. The blood-red windowpanes glowed like the eyes of a hungry cat.

I jumped. Talk about a fur-raising experience!

I headed down a dark corridor. It led to a heavy wooden door. "M-m-may I c-c-come in? Anybody h-h-home?" I stuttered, pushing open the door.

In front of me was a huge room filled with antique furniture. Dust and cobwebs hung over the sofas like unwanted guests the morning after a party. Gigantic paintings of cats from *centuries* long ago covered the walls. I was glad not to be living in that period! Too many cats back then.

Then I noticed a velvet wall hanging with embroidered writing. It read:

This castle belongs to the most honorable Duke Bigpaw Cannycat.

Cannycat? That reminded me of something. I closed my eyes and pictured my precious set of the *Encyclopaedia Ratannica*. Now, what was that I had read about Cannycat??? Oh, yes, of course!

The Cannycats were leaders in the great battle of Raterloo. It took place in 1754. The cats and rats fought courageously with paws and claws. Of course, as every mouse knows, the rodents won. Since Raterloo, there have been no cats on our island.

Just then, I noticed a plaque above the fireplace. I crept closer for a look. My whiskers began to tremble as I read the writing:

"Oh, you foolish rodent who has made it thus far, I bet you don't know how unlucky you are! Retrace your steps and hit the old trail, if you wish to save your miserable tail! Meooow!!!"

Plop!

Now I was shaking all over. I started to back away and bumped into a bookcase. A big fat book landed on my right paw. **Cheese niblets!** That book weighed more than a ten-ton block of cheddar!

Bop!

Bang!

Ouuuuchhhh!!!!!

I shrieked, hopping around like the Easter Rat.

Bam!

Seconds later, I **tripped over** the carpet. I landed snout-first in the fireplace. Now I was covered in ashes from head to tail! How would I explain this mess to Starchette, the cute mouse down at my dry cleaners?

I tried to grab the edge of the fireplace but missed. Instead, I grabbed a doily with a **HEAVY** silver tray on it. The tray bonked me on the head.

Bonk!

Rotten rats' teeth! I was going to have some lump on my head.

I wouldn't be able to wear a hat for weeks! Of course, I never really wear a hat. It would clash with my suit

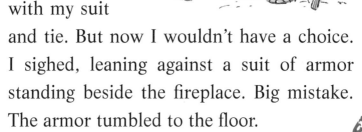

Sigh!

and tie. But now I wouldn't have a choice. I sighed, leaning against a suit of armor standing beside the fireplace. Big mistake. The armor tumbled to the floor.

Whoosh! A sharp hatchet nearly *took off my snout!*

I'M TOO FOND OF MY WHISKERS!!!

Whoosh!

I got up in a daze, trying to steady myself. Then I noticed a mirror over the fireplace. I peered

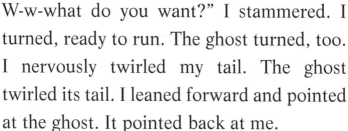

into it. In the dim light, I saw a horrifying sight. **A GHOST WITH A GRAY SNOUT WAS STARING BACK AT ME!**

I let out an ear-splitting squeak! "W-w-who are you? W-w-what do you want?" I stammered. I turned, ready to run. The ghost turned, too. I nervously twirled my tail. The ghost twirled its tail. I leaned forward and pointed at the ghost. It pointed back at me.

"Oops," I mumbled. "That's no ghost. That's just me! How could I be such a nincompoop?"

Oh, how I wished I was home!

Mouse Bones and Rat Skeletons

I left the room and scurried down the hall. Soon I came to a wooden door with a sign on it. It read:

Kitchen

I went in. The place was huge. You could cook dinner for a hundred mice in this place. There was a huge wood-burning stove, pots

and pans of every size and shape, and a massive fridge.

I opened a side door and found myself in a cellar. I spotted some cans of tuna fish, some dried meat, and a big block of **SWISS CHEESE**. It smelled delicious! So the castle was inhabited after all!

But by whom? That was still a mystery.

I crept back to the wood-burning stove. A huge copper pot hung inside the fireplace. It had a picture of a snarling cat engraved on it. I looked closer and noticed a strange white object lying inside the pot.

I picked it up to study it.

"Sour cheese chunks!" It was a **bone** . . . a mouse bone!

I flung the bone back into the pot Then I looked around, terrified. What was this place?

I decided I didn't want to stick around to find out. I had to make a run for it before I ended up like that poor mouse in the pot! No fur, just bone!

In a **panic**, I flung open the first door I saw. Behind it was a closet. I wish I could say I found a puffy chef's hat and matching apron in that closet.

My uncle Hotpaw wears this silly apron at our annual family barbecues.

It has a picture of a smiling mouse juggling kittens on it.

But there was no apron in this closet. Instead, there was the . . .

. . .SKELETON OF A HUMONGOUS RAT!

Oh, how I wished I was home!

I'm Scarier Than Most!

My heart was hammering away like one of those rodents on a mouse hole improvement show. I raced out of the kitchen as fast as my paws could carry me.

I guess you know by now, I'm not the most **COURAGEOUS** mouse on the block.

I scurried into the castle's library. Ah, the library. It really is my favorite place to be. Being a brainy mouse, I love to surround myself with books. Old books, new books — I love them all. Just the smell of a good book is enough to calm me down.

But then I heard it. A strange CREAK from one of the shelves. I stood up and came face-to-face with a ghost! And this was not just any old ghost. It was the GHOST of . . . a cat!

The ghost raced toward me, dragging along a set of chains. It began to meow in a scary voice:

Meoooooowwwwww!
I'm old Slicedpaw's ghost!
I'm scarier than most!
Once you see me, you're toast!
Better head for the coast!
Meoooooowwwwww!
I'm old Slicedpaw's ghost!

I wanted to run. I wanted to hide. I wanted to squeak for my mommy at the top of my lungs. But I was frozen with *fear*!

Just then, I heard another CREAKING sound. As if by magic, the ghost disappeared.

Oh, how I wished I was home!

GERONIMO! QUIT THE HYSTERICS!

I bolted down the hall and flew out the front door. "**HEEEEEEELP!**" I squeaked into the dark, rainy night. But of course, no one answered. How could they? There wasn't a paw or tail in sight. I was alone. Yes, all alone in the spooky Dark Forest. Oh, how I wished I was home! I **SHIVERED**. My whiskers were getting soaked. Now what?

Before I could come up with a plan, my cell phone rang. It was working again! It played classical music. For a minute, I let myself enjoy the soothing sounds of Ratwig van Beethoven. What an amazing composer. Then I remembered where I was and what I had just seen in the castle. "Poisonous cheese puffs!" I shrieked into the phone. "Who is it? You've got to help me!"

It was my sister, Thea. "Geronimo? Where are you? What's going on?" she asked calmly.

I was back in full panic mode. "The b-bone; I mean, the c-castle; ahem, the kitchen; that is, the skeleton and the armor, too, all because of the fog. And I saw a light at the window, but there's n-n-no one here," I stammered. "Holey cheese, I'm scared. Come and save me!!!!!"

My sister sighed. She is the exact opposite of me. That mouse would stay calm even if she got stuck in a tornado and touched down at the Catwalk Seaside

Resort! "Geronimo! Quit the hysterics!" she ordered in her no-nonsense voice. "Now, tell me exactly where you are."

I stared into the dark night. "Um, I don't know, I'm somewhere in the Dark Forest," I began. "I passed Sadsack Point, but I got lost. Then my car broke down, and I found this castle. It's empty, but . . ."

My sister snorted. "Why are you getting your whiskers in a twist, then?" she scolded. "If you are at a castle, just pick a room and hit the sack. Tomorrow morning you can find the main road and go home. Cheese niblets! You really make a mountain out of a mousehill sometimes!"

I peered back at the castle. "But I don't want to sleep here!" I whined. "The castle is empty! It's too scary! And it's **MUCH TOO DARK!**"

Of course, my sister had an answer for

everything. She pointed out that I would not need light since I was going to sleep anyway. Then she called me a 'fraidy mouse. I was insulted. But I was too afraid to say so.

"Is there anything there to eat?" my sister asked. I told her about the cheese I had found in the kitchen.

"That's great! What more do you want?" she demanded. "You're at a c a **s t l e** and you have cheese!"

I reminded her about the mouse **bone** in the kitchen. Not to mention that hideous rat skeleton hanging in the closet.

"Oh, brother, you've got one active imagination," she scoffed. "Bones, skeletons. Maybe you should try cleaning your glasses. Or maybe you should have a little chat with Dr. Shrinkfur. I think you're seeing things!"

I heard the splashing of water. Thea must have been taking her nightly bath. Oh, how I wished I was home in my own bathtub! I could be relaxing in lots of bubbles. I could be playing with my squeaky-cheese bath toy.

Suddenly, a noise interrupted my happy thoughts. It was coming from the big hall inside the castle.

"Listen, Thea," I whispered. **"You won't believe this. But I've just seen a ghost!"**

My sister coughed. "A GHOST? You mean a real GHOST?" she squeaked.

"Yes, it was a real ghost," I repeated. Thea was silent. I knew she was trying to decide if I was telling the truth. I don't know why my family never believes me. I mean, I am a newspaper mouse. I tell it the way I see it.

"Listen, Thea. I know a ghost when I see one," I insisted. "And this was a real honest-to-goodmouse ghost!"

I heard a loud splashing sound. It sounded like my sister was getting out of the tub. Seconds later, she came back on the line. "Well, why didn't you tell me about this ghosty guy in the first place? **WHAT A CHEESEBRAIN!**" she shrieked. Her squeak was earsplitting!

"This could be a great ghost scoop. **I'M ON MY WAY!**" Thea cried. "I'll take pictures. The paper will sell like hot cheesecakes! Bye!"

She slammed down the receiver. I was left listening to the dial tone.

I stared at the castle. It reminded me of when I used to go trick-or-treating as a young mouselet. There was one mouse hole on the block that was supposed to be haunted. My cousin Trap would ring the doorbell. Then we'd all go scampering away. One time, my tail got caught on the front gate. I was never so scared in my whole life. I cried so much my candy got soaking wet. Everyone made fun of me for weeks. It was awful.

Just then, I was hit by a sudden thought.

"Rat-munching rattlesnakes!" I squeaked. "Today is October thirty-first. It's the spookiest day of the year! Halloween!"

Oh, how I wished I was home!

HALLOWEEN!

THE CAT'S EYES

I tried to call my sister back, but I couldn't get through.

What should I do?

I decided to follow her advice and go to bed.

I took a deep breath and headed back into the castle. Then I slowly began to climb up the creaking staircase that led to the upper floor.

I had found a candle in the entrance hall. By the light of the flickering flame, I saw the portraits of the Cannycat family.

I read the names:

Duke Bigpaw Cannycat
Duchess Curlypaw Cannycat
Pinkypaw Cannycat . . .

WHAT A PURRR-fEctly frightening family! At least to a mouse, that is.

Then I passed Duke Slicedpaw Cannycat's portrait. I had the feeling I was being watched. A cold shiver made my fur **STAND ON END.**

I turned around. Nothing.

I crept a little farther. Then I turned around again.

I saw the eyes of Slicedpaw's portrait glow like they were alive. Yes, I was sure of it now. Those eyes were following me as I climbed up the stairs!

I checked the painting. Just as I thought. The eyes had **HOLES** in them! Someone *was* spying on me!

I hurried down the dark hallway. Quickly, I yanked open the first door I saw. I closed it behind me, out of breath.

THE NOBLE
CANNYCAT CLAN

What a day!
What a night!
What a fright!

I stared down at my fur. What mouse bumps! They were popping up all over the place like pimples on a teenage rodent!

I checked out the room I had stumbled into by candlelight. It was painted all black. How dark and depressing. I prefer yellow myself. It's a very cheery color. And of course, it's the color of cheese!

The room was covered in cobwebs. In the center stood a huge four-poster bed. I noticed a name carved on the headboard:

Slicedpaw Cannycat.

There was also a marble fireplace. I

wondered if there were any mouse bones in this one. I shivered. Then I noticed something odd. The room seemed to be connected to a laboratory. It was filled with shelves of books on **magic**. Could Duke Slicedpaw Cannycat have been a magician? I locked the door and pushed a heavy chest of drawers against it. You never can be too safe. Then I lay down on the bed. But my eyes were wide open. In fact, I hadn't blinked for ten minutes! No, I wasn't tired. How could I sleep with a terrifying ghost cat prowling around out there?!

My teeth began to chatter. I had to get my mind off that ghost. I picked up a book on the bedside table.

The title was THE CANNYCAT CLAN TELLS ALL: SECRETS AND SCANDALS OF A NOT-SO-NOBLE FAMILY.

The
Cannycat Clan
Tells All:
Secrets and
Scandals of a
Not-so-noble
Family

As I leafed through the book, I recognized the cats from the portraits I had seen earlier. Curious, I began to read. . . .

PRINCE BIGPAW CANNYCAT
Founder of the Cannycat dynasty. Known to his friends as Bigpaw Poppa.

DUCHESS CURLYPAW CANNYCAT
Famous for her stunning muskrat cape. She ruled the family with an iron curly paw. Meow!

DUKE SLICEDPAW CANNYCAT
His paw was cut off during the battle of Raterloo. It is rumored he could smell a mouse blindfolded in an airtight room with a clothespin stuck on his nose! Legend has it, he was a magician. His ghost wanders around the castle to this day.

DUKE SHORTYPAW CANNYCAT

Nicknamed "Penny-pincher" because of his stinginess. He wore the same underwear for months to save on laundry detergent.

BARONESS PINKYPAW CANNYCAT

The duke's daughter. A beautiful female cat. She married Baron von Slinker and had three kittens: Slinky, Slinkette, and Slinks Cannycat.

DUKE LONGPAW CANNYCAT

Curlypaw's great-grandson. He was known for his expensive tastes. He would only eat at the best fish restaurants in town. He loved gambling and ended up squandering the family fortune.

CREEEAK!

Reading about those Cannycats must have made me sleepy. I dozed off. The next thing I knew, I was woken up by a noise.

CREEEAK! It was coming from the laboratory.

"What's that? Who's there?" I asked, my heart in my mouth.

At first, no one answered. Then I heard it. A chilling, catlike laugh.

"Meooooow . . ." moaned someone at the other end of the room. It was the GHOST!

"Heeeeelp!" I screamed, terrified. I shoved aside the dresser I had used to block the door. Then I slipped out and fled down the hallway.

My heart hammered away in my chest. I felt like it was drilling a hole through hard concrete in there. I raced down the stairs. The creepy portrait of Slicedpaw watched me go.

Suddenly, a bolt of lightning struck close to the castle. The red windowpanes glowed in the darkness. I gasped. A **grim** and horrifying shape stood out against one of the windows. The next moment, it was

Heeeeeelp!

blocking my way. Then it pinched my tail. It shouted, "**Boo!**"

"Thundering cattails!" I shrieked.

What a day! What a night! What mouse bumps!

THEN, OF COURSE, I FAINTED.

TRICKED YOU!
TRICKED YOU!

I came to slowly. Someone was gently slapping my snout.

"The . . . the GHOST . . . Slicedpaw," I murmured.

I opened my eyes and found myself snout-to-snout with my sister, Thea.

She stared down at me curiously. "Did you see the ghost again?" she squeaked. "Where is it? Let me get a picture."

My whiskers were quivering with curiosity. "Y-yes, s-sure, I saw it, all right," I stammered. "It's right here somewhere. It pinched my tail. And this time it shouted **Boo!**"

Just then, I heard someone giggling. I whirled around. It was my cousin Trap.

"Maybe you should get those glasses checked, Cousin," he smirked. "It was me who pinched your tail, not a ghost!"

Now I was fuming. Of all the rotten, low-down, dirty tricks. Only my obnoxious cousin Trap would scare a mouse when he's already frightened!

As I stewed, Trap began to dance around the room. "Tricked you! Tricked you!" he sang in an annoying voice.

Tricked you! Tricked you! Tricked you!

You're Such a
Scaredy Mouse!!!

Right then, someone grabbed my jacket. I looked down. It was *my favorite nephew*, Benjamin.

"Uncle Geronimo! I'm so happy to see you!" he squeaked.

I patted Benjamin's head. "You shouldn't have brought him," I complained to my sister. "Benjamin is much too young. He could get scared!"

My cousin winked at me. "I'm sure he won't get scared. You are the only **scaredy mouse** in the family!" he sneered.

My sister stamped her paw. I could tell she was getting impatient. She wanted to see the ghost, and she wanted to see it now! That sister of mine can't wait for anything.

"Come on, Geronimo," she demanded. "Where is this ghost? I haven't got all day, you know!"

I pulled at my fur. "I'm telling you I saw it with my own eyes!"

I insisted. "And then it suddenly vanished!"

Trap snickered. "Did you see it with your own eyes or with your *four*  *eyes*?" he squeaked. "I mean, you did have your glasses on, right, Cousinkins?"

Then he pinched my tail again.

I tried to catch him. But instead, I Stumbled Over my own two paws.

Oh, how I wished I was home!

THE MYSTERIOUS NAIL

We decided to explore the entire castle.

"We'll catch that ghost," said Thea. "That is . . . if Mr. Scaredy Pants is right and there really is a ghost."

I chewed my whiskers. "I'm telling you for the last time. I saw it! I saw a ghost!!!!!!" I squeaked at the top of my lungs.

Thea pulled out her camera. "All right, all right," she smirked. "Don't have a squeak attack. Now, where did you see that RAT SKELETON? I could take a couple of pictures of that."

I led them into the kitchen. Then I looked anxiously into the big pot.

"See, the mouse bone was here . . ." I began. But the pot was now empty. How strange!

I ran toward the closet and opened it wide. The SKELETON had vanished!!!

I was shocked. "But . . . but . . . it was right here . . ." I mumbled.

Thea snorted.

Trap put his paw on my forehead. "Hmmmm. You're feeling a bit warm, Cousinkins," he joked. "Maybe you're coming down with something. We'd better get you to a hospital. You know, one of those hospitals with bars on the windows and patients who see flying cheeses." He collapsed in a fit of giggles. He really cracks himself up. I wanted to crack him over the head, but before I could even try, Benjamin grabbed my paw.

He showed me a nail in the upper part of the closet. "Um, see that nail, Uncle Geronimo?" he whispered. "There could have been something hanging from it, just like you said. I believe you."

Without another word, he pulled out a pad of paper. Then he began to jot down some notes.

GOT YOU AGAIN!

I didn't feel like exploring the castle anymore. I was tired of being scared out of my fur. All I wanted to do was go home. Home to my cozy mouse hole. Home to my comfy bed. Home to my cheese-filled fridge.

I dragged my paws. "Why don't you go ahead," I told the others. "I'll just wait here."

"Forget it, big brother!" Thea squeaked. "You didn't bring me all the way out here for nothing. I want a ghost! And I want one now! Now, shake your tailfur!"

I sighed. There's no stopping my sister once she wants something. She's like one of those Runaway Ratsy dolls. Turn her on and she's off! Except Thea runs on cheese instead of batteries.

"OK, let's split up," she declared. "I'll cover the kitchen. Trap will take the living room. Benjamin will check out the cellar. And that leaves Geronimo with the library. Let's do it!"

Everyone took off except me. I sighed. Oh, how I hate to be FRIGHTENED. Reluctantly, I headed for the library.

But just as I turned the corner, the ghost appeared in front of me. He was waving his sheet and dancing about. "Woooo!" he moaned in a spooky voice. "I am the castle ghost. Get lost, or you'll be toast!"

My whiskers trembled. "The g-g-ghost . . ." I stammered.

Just then, I heard someone laughing. Of course, I should have guessed who it was. There stood my incredibly irritating cousin Trap. He pulled the sheet off his head and grinned.

"Got you again, didn't I?" he snorted. "You're such a simpleton, Geronimoid!"

My whiskers were trembling again. But this time they weren't trembling with fear. They were trembling with rage!

I jumped to my paws. But before I could squeak, Trap pushed by me. "Catch you later, scaredy mouse!" he called.

My whiskers sagged. So much for squeaking my mind. Oh, well, there was no time to worry about my rotten cousin now.

Ancient Roman cat

Barbarian cat

I decided to check out the library. Books spilled out from the shelves. I read some of the titles. *A Purrfect Place: If Cats Ruled the World; Don't Step in My Litter Box!; How to Catnap and Still Lose Weight.* There was also a book on the history of cats. On the front it had pictures of cats from different periods of history.

Shivering, I put the book back on the shelf. I was starting to get a funny feeling about this castle. There were no cats left on Mouse Island . . . were there?

Medieval cat

17th-century cat

I pulled another book from the shelf. It was called *One Hundred Easy Ways to Cook a Rat*.

I gasped. Then I flipped through the recipes.

Sweet and sour mouse skewers

Grilled rat with herbs

Mouse marrow soup

Peppery rodent casserole

Chocolate cake supreme with candied rat tails

My fur stood on end. Maybe the rat skeleton I saw in the kitchen closet was left over from some crazy cat's casserole!

THE MYSTERY OF THE VANISHING GHOST

Suddenly, I heard a noise coming from behind a bookshelf.

MeeeeeeeeooooOOOOwwwwwiiiMMMMMM

"Meeooww!!!" a voice sang out.

I snorted. This time I wasn't falling for it. I'd had enough of my cousin's silly jokes. I didn't even look up.

The meowing continued.

"Enough, Trap," I mumbled. "I know it's you."

Then I heard a CREEAAAK.

I lifted my snout, ready to give my cousin a piece of my mind.

But instead, I jumped so high my fur nearly brushed the ceiling! "Cheese niblets!"

In front of me stood the ghost!

It was dressed in a suit of metal armor. It had the head of a cat, and one of its paws was missing. Yes, this time I was certain. It *was* Slicedpaw's ghost! It was as PALE as a slice of mozzarella. But this was no giant talking piece of cheese! It was an honest-to-goodmouse ghost!

Oh, how I wished I was home!

Right then, the ghost slipped behind a bookshelf.

Once again, I heard a

CREEAAAK . . . .

I'll Tear Out Your Whiskers!!!

I ran into the hall. "Heeeeelp!!! Someone save me! There's a g-ghost!!!" I shrieked. I was so nervous, I twisted my tail into a knot.

Then I felt a paw on my shoulder. It was a cold, furry paw. The ghost! It had me in its catty clutches! Oh, what a sad and scary way to go. "Good-bye, Thea! Good-bye, Benjamin! Good-bye, cruel world!" I sobbed.

But the ghost just snorted. That's because it wasn't really a ghost at all. "It's just me!" Thea yelled in my ear. Her whiskers were *twitching twitching twitching twitching twitching twitching* from excitement. "Now, stop whining and tell me where this ghost is!"

But I was so worked up, I could hardly think. "The g- ghost . . . All W-W-WHITE . . . A c-c-cut-off paw . . ." I stammered.

My sister tapped her paw impatiently. "Yes, but where?" she insisted. "Where did you see it? **WHERE?**"

In a daze, I stared back at her. She grabbed me by the tie, trying to shake the information out of me. Did I mention my sister can be a little impatient?

At last, my squeak returned. I told her about the library. I told her how the ghost had appeared from behind a bookshelf.

She grabbed her camera and was off. I followed her. But when we reached the library, it was empty. Not a ghost in sight.

"I saw it! I'm positive!" I kept repeating.
I heard a **chuckle** from behind me. It
was Trap. "I saw it, I
saw it!" he sang in a
high-pitched voice.

"Geronimoid, how
many paws am I
holding up? Do
you see what
color shirt I am
wearing? Do you see little green mice
floating above my head?" He cackled with
laughter. "No? But you see a GHOST?"

I was furious. Thea was furious, too. The
only problem was, she was furious with me!
"Geronimooo!" she squeaked, stamping her
paw. "One more joke like this and I'll tear
out all of your whiskers!"

I started to protest, but then I gave up. It

was no use. Why, oh, why did no one ever believe me?

Just then, Benjamin rushed to my side. "If Uncle Geronimo says he saw it, I'm sure he **DID**!" he cried.

But no one paid any attention to him. So Benjamin began to examine the library's floor.

"What's up, Benjamin? Did you find something?" I asked.

He pointed to some marks on the wooden floor. They looked like Scratches. Maybe marks made by the ghost's chains?

I saw Benjamin pull out his pad. Without a word, he began to jot down some notes.

AH, THESE
BRAINY MICE . . .

It was very late. I wanted to go to bed. I was exhausted. But my sister wouldn't let me.

"I need to get a picture of that ghost," she insisted. "Ghosts wander around at **NIGHT**, not in the middle of the day, you cheesebrain! If you really saw a ghost, you'd help me find him!"

"What does he know about ghosts," Trap said smugly. "I think Gerry Berry just ate too much cheese. Then he had a **NIGHTMARE** and saw a ghost. Everyone knows that brainy mice have **wild** imaginations."

He pinched my tail. "Got to get your nose out of those books, Gerrykins!" he shrieked. "You're seeing **too many** ghosts. . . ."

I rubbed my tail. *That's it,* I decided. I'd had enough of the Stilton family for one night.

"I'm going to bed!" I announced. I headed for Slicedpaw's room and I slammed the door behind me.

I had just stretched out on the bed when I heard a sound. CREEEEEAK!

Then I heard a loud meowing.

Slicedpaw's white ghost jumped out from behind the bookshelf! It sneered at me.

Once again, I was trembling with fear. That ghost must have been following me! Why was it picking on me? Did it know I was really a scaredy mouse at heart? Did it know I still slept with my Cheeseball the Clown night-light on?

"Heeeeeeeeelp!" I screamed at the top of my lungs. "It's back! The ghost is back!"

Oh, how I wished I was home!

In a flash, my sister stormed into the room. "WHERE IS IT? WHERE IS IT THIS TIME?" she shouted.

I pointed toward the bookshelf.

But just like before, it had vanished!

Thea was beside herself with rage. Her whiskers stood on end. Steam poured out of her ears.

"Enough is enough, Geronimo! I don't like to be tricked," she squeaked. "One more time and that ghost won't be the only one around here who's missing a paw!"

Trap sniggered behind his whiskers. Meanwhile, Benjamin pointed out a line of white powder on the floor. It was close to the bookshelf. I sniffed it. How very strange. It was *flour!*

Once again, Benjamin jotted some notes onto his pad.

THE MUMMY INSIDE
THE COFFIN

I decided to sleep in another room. I took a pillow and a blanket. Then I crept downstairs to the cellar.

Ah, peace and quiet at last. I fell asleep in an instant.

I was happily snoring away when I heard that creaking sound.

CREEEAAAK . . .

I woke up with a start.

I lit the candle beside me.

"Is that you, Benjamin?" I asked in a shaky voice.

No one answered.

I lifted the candle so I could see better.

Then I saw it. My eyes popped open wide.

It was a **MUMMY!** And it was staggering right toward me!

Behind it stood an open coffin made of stone.

For the millionth time that night, I cried out. "Help . . . heeeelp!" I yelled as loud as I could. My voice echoed in the dark, empty room.

Oh, how I wished I was home!

Thea was beside me in no time flat. "Well, what is it this time?" she asked warily.

I puffed up my fur. Now my sister would see I was telling the truth. After all, a mummy is a mummy. You can't make that up. "Go ahead," I announced, standing up tall. "Take a look over there. Well, what do you see?"

I expected my sister to whip out her camera. I expected her to gasp with surprise. Instead, she closed her eyes. Then she shrieked, "I don't see a thing!!!"

I turned around, astonished. The mummy and the coffin had both vanished!

I went to check. No trace of them near the *suit of armor*. Nothing!

"I-I can't believe it! This just isn't possible," I stammered, confused.

Thea grabbed me by the ear. "First it's a ghost, now it's a mummy. What's next, a fire-breathing dragon?" she hissed.

Benjamin was busy checking out the room. He showed me a piece of toilet paper. It was stuck on the floor right where I had seen the mummy. Strange.

Without a word, Benjamin pulled out his pad. Then he jotted down some notes.

DON'T MESS
WITH MOMMA!

I took my things and scuttled away, quiet as a mouse.

Oh, how I wished I was home!

As I left, I heard my cousin giggling. "What a wacko," he sputtered. "That mouse is going to end up on the funny farm for sure!"

My whiskers were quivering with rage. How dare he call me a wacko!

I've seen those mice at the Mad Mouse Center. And let me tell you, I do not act like them! Oh, sure, some of them are a little on the jumpy side, just like me. And yes, some of them claim to have seen things like ghosts and mummies, just like me. And some of them may even be afraid of heights

and spiders and electric toothbrushes and cotton candy (it gets stuck in the whiskers) and . . . well, you get the idea. But I am not like them! *I am a mouse of honor!* Holding my candle high, I crept slowly down the dark hallway. I was so frightened. I blinked rapidly to keep from crying my eyes out.

Finally, I came to a room wallpapered with yellow roses. It was double the size of the other bedrooms. The four-poster bed was HUGE. My whole family, including my

chubby uncle Cheesebelly, could have slept in it! The drapes had the same pretty yellow roses on them. Too bad it looked as if someone had slashed them with a knife. Still, the room was quite spectacular. And it even smelled like roses.

Above the fireplace hung a huge portrait with a golden frame. It showed *Duchess Curlypaw Cannycat*. She was surrounded by her children, grandchildren, and great-grandchildren. By the look on her face, you could tell she was the true ruler of the

Cannycat clan. On a chest of drawers stood a marble bust of the duchess. She wore a superior smile on her furry face. It was engraved:

DON'T MESS WITH MOMMA!

A miniature reproduction of the castle stood on the bedside table. I bent closer to get a better look. Etched into the silver were the words CURLYPAW CANNYCAT'S CASTLE.

I was right. It seemed the duchess had been the ruler of the castle. I had a feeling she ruled with an iron paw!

On the walls hung letters from the most famous cats of

the time. There were letters from grand dukes, kings, even emperors. I was impressed. 𝕯uchess 𝕮urlypaw 𝕮annycat was no kitty.

She also had expensive tastes. I saw lots of gold and precious jewels on her many bureaus. On one stood a heavy golden birdcage with a bird tweeting in the center. On another, I spotted a magnificent solid-gold crown. It was set with rubies as big as cats' eyes. This must have been the duchess's crown!

Then I spotted a TINY gold figurine. It was a shy, timid-looking cat. A little plaque underneath the figurine read:

MY DECEASED HUSBAND
DUKE PEEWEE PUNYPAW (1720–1760)

Well, that explains it, I thought.

Curlypaw Cannycat was a widow. That's why she ruled over the castle and the family.

I also found a dusty small pillow. It was decorated with tiny yellow roses and the words:

Momma is the ruler around this place, so do as she says . . . or she'll rearrange your face!

A MYSTERIOUS REFLECTION

I put out the candle and slipped under the covers.

I closed my eyes. But one horrible thought kept popping up. Tonight was *Halloween.* The scariest night of the year! Did I mention I don't like to be scared?

Get a grip, Geronimo, I told myself sharply. It's time to stop being such a scaredy mouse. Yes, I, *Geronimo Stilton*, would turn over a new leaf. From now on, I would be brave. To give myself courage, I began to chant, "I am not a scaredy mouse. I am not a scaredy mouse." I repeated the words over and over like a CD stuck on REPEAT. After a while, my paws stopped shaking. I peeked out from under the covers. I was starting to feel better. I guess you could even say I felt stronger, tougher. No ghost was going to send this mouse scampering. In fact, I would just laugh in his ghosty old face.

Then I heard a CREEEaAAK.

A meowing voice called out into the dark room. "That's right," it said. "You're not a scaredy mouse. You're a terrified mouse! He-he-he... He-he-he... He-he-he... He-he-he!" My fur stood on end with fright. "Who . . . who's there???" I squeaked.

Oh, how I wished I was home!

A light came on in the **DARKEST** corner of the room, by a small bookshelf. There I saw a female figure wearing a cone-shaped hat, a long black dress, and pointed shoes.

"I am not a scaredy mouse."

She held a broom in her paw. Could it be a witch's broom? Her wide-brimmed hat covered her snout, but I could tell she was a cat.

The paw holding the broom had long, sharp claws. Brrrrrrrrr!

Poisonous cheesy puffs! It was a **witch**. And not just any old witch. The worst kind of witch there is. A CAT witch!

I stared at her frightening reflection in the mirror.

The witch began to chuckle. Then she sang a horrifying song.

"Evil eye and rodent's pie, in my cauldron prepare to die!" she cackled. She waved her broom in the air. "Well, well, well . . . what a nice, juicy mouse. You'd be just right for a couple of ratburgers. I could use that fur to make myself a cute hat. And those soft little ears would make a perfect powder puff!

He-he-he... He-he-he... He-he-he... He-he-he."

I hid under the covers. So much for being brave. I admit it. I am a scaredy mouse. A perfectly terrified, teeth-chattering, nail-biting scaredy mouse!

"Heeeeeelp!" I shrieked once again. I was beginning to sound like a broken record.

Thirty seconds later, Thea threw open the door.

"What's up? Did you see a ghost?" she cried.

I shook my head. "No," I squeaked. "I saw a **witch!**"

My sister blinked. Then she flipped her tail over her shoulder. "Well, it doesn't really matter, I suppose. A witch would make a good scoop, too," she decided. "So where is she?"

Trembling all over, I pointed at the bookshelf. Armed with her camera, my sister marched forward.

I watched as she stared at the bookshelf. "Where are you, Witch?" she demanded. "Come on, I just want to take your picture."

I peeked out from under the covers. I was shaking like a mouse who's been locked out of his or her mouse hole on a cold winter's night.

Thea looked everywhere. But the witch was **GONE!**

I LOVE YOU,
UNCLE GERONIMO!

My sister stamped over to the bed. She ripped the covers off me.

"Geronimo!" she barked. "How much cheese did you eat tonight?"

I chewed my whiskers. "V-very little, I'm telling you!" I insisted.

Just then, Trap peeked into the room. "Very little, my paw," he chuckled. "He probably ate so much, his stomach begged him to stop. You know, Gerry Berry, you can have terrible nightmares when you eat **too much** before bed." He poked me in the tummy. "You probably dreamed up all sorts of scary thingies, like ghosts and mummies and witches."

I shook my head. Why wouldn't anyone ever *listen* to me? "For the last time, I'm telling you. I only ate a tiny piece of Swiss cheese!" I squeaked.

Of course, that got Trap started on the dangers of going to bed on an empty stomach. "That's even worse than eating **too much!**" he shouted.

Meanwhile, Benjamin was checking out the mirror, the walls, and a chest of drawers standing in the dark corner of the room.

He scratched the fur on top of his head. "Tell me, Uncle," he whispered in my ear.

"Are you positive you saw the witch **reflected in that mirror?**"

I nodded. "You do believe me, don't you?" I asked my *favorite* nephew.

Benjamin kissed me on the tip of my snout.

"OF COURSE I BELIEVE YOU, UNCLE! I ALWAYS DO!"

I hugged him tight.

Then he pulled out his pad. Without another word, he jotted down some notes.

"Of course I believe you, Uncle!"

SMALL BUT NASTY!!!

Finally, they all left. I sat on the bed, thinking. What was going on? Was I just having nightmares, like Trap insisted? Or did I actually see a ghost, a mummy, and now a witch? I was starting to feel like I was losing my mind!

To cheer myself up, I started chanting again: **"EVERYTHING'S UNDER CONTROL! EVERYTHING'S UNDER CONTROL!"** But this time, I didn't feel any better.

Oh, how I wished I was home!

Suddenly, a gray owl flew into the room through the open window. It perched on the edge of the fireplace.

The owl opened its beak. "Hey you, cheddarface!" it croaked.

My jaw dropped.
Then the owl began to sing:

"I may be small,
But don't cross me.
One wrong move
And you're history!"

It left in a **WHIRL** of feathers.

As the owl flew away, I heard a mechanical sound. tick **-tack** tick **-tack**. *How very strange,* I thought. I wanted to tell someone. Whoever heard of a talking owl? And not just any talking owl. This was one *nasty* talking owl! I opened my mouth to yell for help.

Then I snapped it shut. Why bother? No one would believe me anyway. They'd call me a cheesebrain. They'd call me a mad mouse. They'd call me for advice and do the exact opposite of whatever I said. No, no one would believe me. Well, no one except Benjamin.

I scrambled out of bed.

Then I raced out of the room in search of my dear, sweet nephew.

THE MYSTERY OF THE CHICKEN FEATHER

I found Benjamin and told him what had happened. He listened patiently.

Then he gave me a hug. "I believe you, Uncle!" he said.

Did I mention Benjamin is my favorite nephew?

We went back to Duchess Curlypaw Cannycat's room. Benjamin began to check out the room like a regular mouse detective.

He found a feather on the floor by the fireplace. He stared at it through a magnifying glass. "Very interesting," he murmured. "This looks like it was a white chicken feather. But someone has painted it **GRAY**."

I told Benjamin about the strange mechanical noise I had heard when the owl flew off.

Tick-tack!
Tick-tack! Tick-tack!

He pointed out the cobwebs over the fireplace. "So many cobwebs, yet not one single spider," he observed. We both agreed it was very odd.

With that, Benjamin pulled out his pad. Then he began scribbling more notes. At this rate, he was going to need another pad!

A SCARLET SILK CAPE

It was already morning. But it felt like midnight. Being haunted by ghosts was exhausting! I hadn't slept one wink.

I decided to try to catch a quick mouse nap. I'd skip Curlypaw's room, though . . . *brrrr!* Instead, I climbed up the stairs leading to the highest tower. Soon I found myself in a **red** room. The walls were **red**. The floor was **red**. Even the ceiling was **red**.

I fell onto the bed. I was so tired. Before my fur even hit the **red** velvet pillow, I was fast asleep.

A few minutes later, I woke up to a strange buzzing sound.

I opened my eyes. Shadows danced on the high ceiling.

Cheese niblets!

They were bat **shadows!**

Oh, how I wished I was home!

Suddenly, one of the shadows drifted over to the bed. It was much, much bigger than the others.

The buzzing whirred in my ears. Just then, the shadow unfolded its wings. I saw a figure cloaked in a scarlet silk cape. It was a

vampire cat! It smiled at me, showing every one of its pointed teeth!

"**A VAMPIIRE!**" I shrieked.

In a flash, it disappeared. The door flew open. It was Benjamin.

"Uncle! Uncle! What's the matter?" he cried, racing to my side.

"I heard a b-b-b-buzzing sound and I saw b-b-bat shadows on the ceiling," I stammered. "Then a vampire appeared at the foot of my bed!"

Benjamin twirled his whiskers. "Hmm. A buzzing sound? Shadows on the ceiling? A vampire?" he said, looking puzzled. Then he glanced out the window. "Look, Uncle, the sun is already up," he pointed out. "I thought vampires slept during the day and came out at night."

I wasn't an expert on vampires. I tried not to read too many spooky books. They were just so scary. But I did know Benjamin was right. Nighttime was a vampire's party hour. Daytime was for sleeping.

Benjamin discovered an extension cord lying on the floor. He held it up for me to see. Once again, we both agreed something very odd was going on.

Benjamin scribbled away on his pad.

AN EXTENSION CORD

? PRANKY PAWS

I was still sleepy. But it didn't look like I'd be catching any Z's until I got home. Then I'd curl up in my comfy bed and sleep for hours. Maybe even days! I would just take a vacation from work. Lately, I'd been working my paws to the bone. A little time off might be just what I needed.

Oh, how I wished I was home!

I **SIGHED**. Then I headed downstairs

with Benjamin. And that's when I saw it. A small tag lay crumpled on the stairs. I picked it up and read it out loud:

PRANKY PAWS
SUPER SCARY
HALLOWEEN
MAGIC TRICKS AND
PRACTICAL JOKES

My mouth dropped open.

"Uncle, are you thinking what I'm thinking?" Benjamin whispered.

I nodded. "Yes, my dear nephew," I murmured. "**Someone** has been playing tricks on us!"

Benjamin took out his pad. On it he had drawn a map of Cannycat Castle. "Maybe we can find out more from this map," he began. We put our heads together and studied the castle.

CANNYCAT CASTLE

1. *Cat statues*
2. *Entrance hall*
3. *Ballroom*
4. *Terrace*
5. *Turret*
6. *Garden*
7. *Vegetable garden*
8. *Conservatory*
9. *Stairs*
10. *Kitchen*
11. *Turret*
12. *Library*
13. *Stairs on upper floor*
14. *Cellar*
15. *Slicedpaw Cannycat's room*
16. *Slicedpaw's laboratory*
17. *Curlypaw Cannycat's room*
18. *Longpaw Cannycat's room*
19. *Pinkypaw Cannycat's room*

THE MYSTERY IS SOLVED

It didn't take long for Benjamin and me to figure everything out.

We called Thea and Trap. Then we all gathered in the library.

"Benjamin and I have finally solved this 𝔪𝔶𝔰𝔱𝔢𝔯𝔶," I announced.

Thea looked puzzled.

Trap just smirked. "What mystery? The mystery of your missing brain cells?" he chuckled.

I ignored him. *We'll see who has the last laugh,* I thought.

I picked up Benjamin's pad and flipped through it. I was so proud of my nephew. His notes were like a regular detective's. I felt like I was reading the journal of that famous TV detective Snoop Rat Smith.

"Let's go over everything that happened from the beginning," I said. I was starting to feel like a detective myself. I paced back and forth for effect. I twirled my whiskers and peered at everyone through a magnifying glass.

Thea rolled her eyes. But for once, no one said a word. Except me. I read the list of points Benjamin and I had gone over in my best Snoop Rat Smith imitation:

1. I discover a rat skeleton in the kitchen cupboard. When Thea shows up, the skeleton disappears. But that's when Benjamin notices the mysterious nail. Why is there a nail in the cupboard? **To hang the skeleton on, of course!**

2. The ghost appears for the first time in the library behind a bookshelf. Whenever the ghost appears and disappears, there is a creaking noise. **That's because there is a secret passageway behind the shelf!**

3. I notice the eyes in Slicedpaw's portrait seem to be following me. It turns out the painting has two holes where the eyes should be! **Someone *has* been watching me!**

4. The ghost appears again in Slicedpaw's lab. Once again, it pops up from behind a bookshelf. **Another secret passageway!**

5. The ghost appears once more in the library. Benjamin notices some marks on the floor. **What kind of ghost can leave a mark? Not a real one!**

6. The ghost reappears. **But this time, Benjamin notices a trace** of flour on the floor!

7. A mummy appears in the cellar. Benjamin finds a piece of toilet paper. What's the easiest way to dress up as a mummy? **Wrap yourself in toilet paper!**

8. A witch appears in Curlypaw's room. **What kind of witch can see her own reflection in the mirror? Not a real one!**

9. A talking owl pays me a visit. But I hear a motor when it flies off. Then Benjamin discovers a painted chicken feather. What kind of owl has a motor and painted feathers? **A mechanical one!**

10. Bat shadows appear and then a vampire. But what is that strange buzzing sound? And why does Benjamin discover an extension cord? Because nothing is real. **They are just images projected on the wall! Plus, every mouse knows real vampires go into hiding when the sun rises.**

11. I discover a strange tag on the stairs. It says,

PRANKY PAWS
SUPER SCARY
HALLOWEEN
MAGIC TRICKS AND
PRACTICAL JOKES.

I put down Benjamin's pad. "So you see," I finished, "someone has been playing tricks on us. They want us to think this castle is haunted. Now we just have to find out **who** and **why!**"

WHAT'S YOUR STORY?

By now, Trap was on his paws. "What?" he squeaked. "Are you telling me that someone has been playing games with us? Messing with our mouse minds? Pulling the wool over our beady little eyes?" He was furious. *"What kind of low-down, slimy sewer rat would do something so nasty?"* he shrieked. "Wait till I get my paws on him. I'll tear out his whiskers one by one!"

Thea was just as furious. "I'll tie his tail in knots!" she squeaked.

Just then, I heard a noise from behind the bookshelf. I leaped toward the shelf *faster than a cat in a rat race*. "You won't get away this time!" I cried.

But when I saw who had been making the

noise, my jaw hit the ground. No, this time I wasn't frightened. I wasn't even scared. I was just surprised. That's because there wasn't a mouse behind the bookshelf. There was a teeny, tiny cat! Now, I know what you're thinking, *Aren't all cats scary to mice?* Well, not this little guy. He was not much older than Benjamin, and he looked like he was about to faint. He was clearly terrified of *us*!

In a flash, Trap snatched him up by the tail.

"Well then, what's your story, Fluffy Fur?" he sneered. "What's with the magic tricks?"

The young cat coughed. He was so frightened, I could hear his teeth chattering. "W-w-well, you see . . ." he began with a stammer.

PAWKIN AND PAWETTE

At last, we learned the little cat's story. It turns out his name was Pawkin Cannycat. He lived in the castle with his sister, Pawette. They were the only descendants of the Cannycat clan. "Since we're on our own, life hasn't been easy," Pawkin explained. "The castle is big and needs lots of repairs. But we don't have the money to fix them. Lots of slimy salescats have tried to get us to sell the castle. But we don't want to sell our family home! It means everything to us!"

I had to smile. For a cat so young, Pawkin had a great sense of family pride.

"I am sorry I played those spooky tricks

on you," the cat went on. "We've been keeping unwanted visitors away by pretending this place is *haunted*."

I put my paw on Pawkin's shoulder. Who would have thought such a timid cat could have given me such a big scare? I guess it's true what they say. You can't judge a book by its cover. Unless, of course, it's a book by *Geronimo Stilton*. All of my books have wonderful covers. And, as you can see, they are very exciting to read.

I told Pawkin not to worry. I would be glad to help him and his sister. After all, I, *Geronimo Stilton*, am a mouse of honor. I always defend the weak and those in need of help.

Suddenly, Thea danced over to Pawkin. "I have a great idea!" she announced. "Why don't we turn your castle into a mouseum/

theme park? The visitors can learn about the history of the Cannycat family and you can perform your scary Halloween tricks. You can have a ghost pop out of the library. A mummy in the cellar. A witch in the bedroom . . ."

The little cat grinned from ear to ear. "I love it!" he purred. "Let me introduce you to my sister."

With that, he pulled out a book from the shelf behind him.

Suddenly, the whole bookcase began to move. A small **female cat** stepped out from a secret passageway.

Who says a cat and a mouse can't be friends?

She looked just like Pawkin.

"Good morning. My name is Pawette Cannycat," she meowed politely.

Benjamin smiled at the tiny cat. "WOULD YOU SHOW ME AROUND THE CASTLE?" he asked.

Pawette smiled back. "I'd love to!" she purred. Soon, Pawette and Benjamin were happily chatting away. I watched as they headed down the hall, holding paws. I grinned.

Who says a cat and a mouse can't be *friends?*

Halloween, a Year Later!!!

A year has gone by since that crazy Halloween night. Lots of things have happened since.

Cannycat Castle has been completely repaired. Every day, there is a line of visitors clamoring to get in. They come to see the beautiful portraits. The antique furniture. The precious jewelry. But most of all, they come to see Pawkin's spooky Halloween magic tricks, Duke Slicedpaw Cannycat's ghost, the mummy, the witch, and the vampire!

Pawkin and Pawette Cannycat are two happy cats. Which reminds me. They have become Benjamin's best friends.

As I was saying, today is October thirty-first. Yes, it's *Halloween.*

My family and I are on our way to Cannycat Castle. We're going to spend the night. It has become a Stilton family tradition.

Benjamin is super excited. He has been telling me about all of the new scary tricks Pawkin has created. Glow-in-the-dark skeletons, headless ghosts, werecats. It all sounds terribly frightening. Of course, I wouldn't tell anyone I am afraid. They would just call me a scaredy mouse.

Which really isn't very nice. But I will tell you a little secret. It is true. I hate ghosts and goblins and haunted houses and things that go squeak in the night. Yes, I admit it. I am a scaredy mouse. A perfectly terrified, teeth-chattering, nail-biting scaredy mouse!

Oh, how I wish I was home!

ABOUT THE AUTHOR

Born in New Mouse City, Mouse Island, Geronimo Stilton is Rattus Emeritus of Mousomorphic Literature and of Neo-Ratonic Comparative Philosophy. For the past twenty years, he has been running *The Rodent's Gazette*, New Mouse City's most widely read daily newspaper.

Stilton was awarded the Ratitzer Prize for his scoop on *The Curse of the Cheese Pyramid*. He has also received the Andersen 2000 Prize for Personality of the Year. One of his bestsellers won the 2002 eBook Award for world's best ratlings' electronic book. His works have been published in 180 countries.

In his spare time, Mr. Stilton collects antique cheese rinds and plays golf. But what he most enjoys is telling stories to his nephew Benjamin.

Don't miss any of my fabumouse adventures!

Want to read my next adventure?
It's sure to be a fur-raising experience!

FOUR MICE DEEP IN THE JUNGLE

I have never been a brave mouse . . . but lately, my fears were taking over my life! Soon I was too afraid even to leave my mouse hole. That's when Thea and Trap decided to cure me. They dragged me away on an airplane (I'm afraid of flying!) all the way to the jungle. There I was forced to eat bug soup, climb trees as high as skyscrapers, swim in raging rivers, and even wrangle snakes! How would a 'fraidy mouse like me ever survive?

THE RODENT'S GAZETTE

1. **Main Entrance**
2. **Printing presses (where the books and newspaper are printed)**
3. **Accounts department**
4. **Editorial room (where the editors, illustrators, and designers work)**
5. **Geronimo Stilton's office**
6. **Storage space for Geronimo's books**

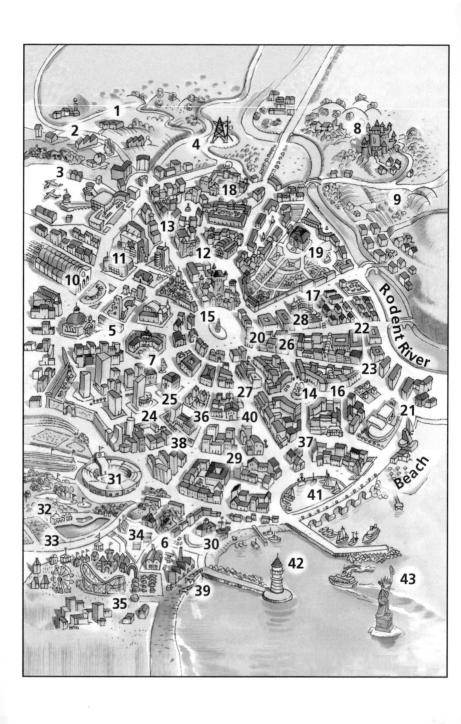

Rodent River

Beach

Map of New Mouse City

1. Industrial Zone
2. Cheese Factories
3. Angorat International Airport
4. WRAT Radio and Television Station
5. Cheese Market
6. Fish Market
7. Town Hall
8. Snotnose Castle
9. The Seven Hills of Mouse Island
10. Mouse Central Station
11. Trade Center
12. Movie Theater
13. Gym
14. Catnegie Hall
15. Singing Stone Plaza
16. The Gouda Theater
17. Grand Hotel
18. Mouse General Hospital
19. Botanical Gardens
20. Cheap Junk for Less (Trap's store)
21. Parking Lot
22. Mouseum of Modern Art
23. University and Library
24. *The Daily Rat*
25. *The Rodent's Gazette*
26. Trap's House
27. Fashion District
28. The Mouse House Restaurant
29. Environmental Protection Center
30. Harbor Office
31. Mousidon Square Garden
32. Golf Course
33. Swimming Pool
34. Blushing Meadow Tennis Courts
35. Curlyfur Island Amusement Park
36. Geronimo's House
37. New Mouse City Historic District
38. Public Library
39. Shipyard
40. Thea's House
41. New Mouse Harbor
42. Luna Lighthouse
43. The Statue of Liberty

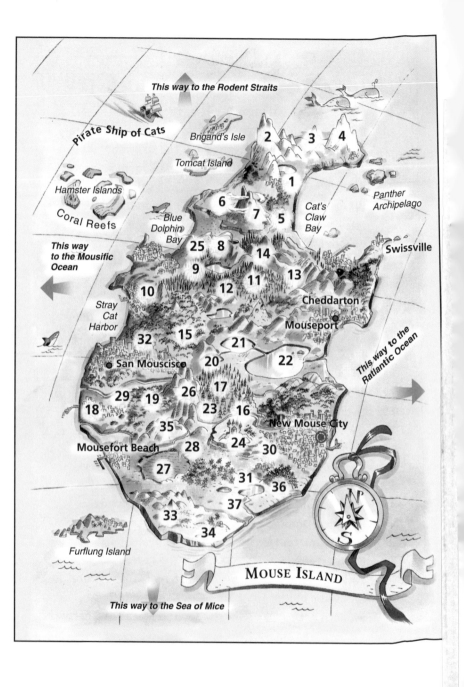

Map of Mouse Island

1. Big Ice Lake
2. Frozen Fur Peak
3. Slipperyslopes Glacier
4. Coldcreeps Peak
5. Ratzikistan
6. Transratania
7. Mount Vamp
8. Roastedrat Volcano
9. Brimstone Lake
10. Poopedcat Pass
11. Stinko Peak
12. Dark Forest
13. Vain Vampires Valley
14. Goose Bumps Gorge
15. The Shadow Line Pass
16. Penny Pincher Lodge
17. Nature Reserve Park
18. Las Ratayas Marinas
19. Fossil Forest
20. Lake Lake
21. Lake Lake Lake
22. Lake Lakelakelake
23. Cheddar Crag
24. Cannycat Castle
25. Valley of the Giant Sequoia
26. Cheddar Springs
27. Sulfurous Swamp
28. Old Reliable Geyser
29. Vole Vail
30. Ravingrat Ravine
31. Gnat Marshes
32. Munster Highlands
33. Mousehara Desert
34. Oasis of the Sweaty Camel
35. Cabbagehead Hill
36. Tropical Jungle
37. Rio Mosquito

Dear mouse friends,
thanks for reading, and farewell
till the next book.
It'll be another whisker-licking-good
adventure, and that's a promise!

Geronimo Stilton